D0881296

SPLENDIDE-HÔTEL

Other Books by Gilbert Sorrentino

SPLENDIDE-
HÔTEL

BY
GILBERT SORRENTINO

AN AFTERWORD

BY

ROBERT CREELEY

Dalkey Archive Press
Fairchild Hall / ISU
Normal, IL 61761
(309) 438-7555

THE DALKEY ARCHIVE PRESS

LIBRARY OF CONGRESS CATALOGING IN PUBLICATION DATA

Sorrentino, Gilbert, 1929-
  Splendide-hôtel.
  I. Title
PS3569.07S6 1984   818'.5407   84-3228
ISBN 0-916583-00-7
ISBN 0-916583-01-5

THE DALKEY ARCHIVE PRESS
1817 N. 79th Avenue
Elmwood Park IL 60635

TO MY OLD FRIEND
HUBERT SELBY

Et le Splendide-Hôtel fut bâti dans le chaos de glaces et de nuit du pôle.

ARTHUR RIMBAUD

"A tall man, dressed rather shabbily, was walking down the road." Thus, any story. The writer wishes to make his sense exact. A . . . what? "A dog came out of the bushes at the side of the road" (in South Newington, New Hampshire) "to confront the man and his wife, halfway to the roadside vegetable stand." The corn there sweet and luscious, kernels popped between the teeth, their sugary juice. It is this letter which serves so well, A. But don't misunderstand me: I am not a "country" writer, although its peace is appealing to me.

The writer—a writer wishes to make his sense exact, or why bother? Precise registrations are beautiful, indeed. The popular novelist deals with feathery edges, one gets a "tone." One gets a "feeling." Then there are those who rhyme dialogue, subsidized assassins of the precise. The inane, the poets in constant residence. They demand of the poem that it adjust their very lives, they die fragmented at parties, turn out bands of students armed against ignorance with error. Error sharpened and ready for assault! Give them annual prizes, I beg you. Beware the interested academic. "A" young English instructor . . . ignorant, ignorant.

In New Hampshire, I dug 280 clams in Portsmouth Bay in 45 minutes. The earth's plenty. My wife made a magnificent clam soup and we had four guests. The children played in the soft night among pines. I was a vacationer. The next day swam in the icy Atlantic, yet knew what I am. From this head —comes beauty. It is the artist who lives the nonartistic life who is most aware of his painfully absurd position. To keep one's mouth shut. Who the hell does he think he is, anyway? One sees in the letter A a constant: and yet, a continuing rejuvenation.

A continuing rejuvenation? Of flies! *Mouches éclatantes.* The poet has it that this primal vowel is black. The great alpha, black A. "Black velvet coat of glittering flies." Black, black. The A, sitting quietly on the page, wings folded back over the shining body. A, a fly. AA, two flies. "It is true that most of them breed in decaying organic matter of some kind, but we must remember that disgust is purely a human reaction."

7

In New Hampshire, a genus of biting fly (*Chrysops*) was so persistent that it would stay on the flesh until the exact moment one sank beneath the water, and sometimes even went under in its ravenous feeding. In this sentence, eleven instances of sudden blackness. Eleven flies.

```
            A A
              A AA    A
      A
        A           A
                    A A
```

A continuing rejuvenation. Thus it is that one often comes across a line of startling beauty and brilliance in an otherwise putrescent poem or page of prose. Movement of the line, its quantity, the shifting of the vowels, the A's breeding in decay. One must read with care, searching for precise registrations. The true poet will always have something to offer. In his lines aspects of the persistent, the re-created. So that these precise notations die only when the world dies. The A waits calmly, shadowing the line. Calm.

To keep one's mouth shut, or, opening it, to see the language in air, inexact somehow. Talking to the young English instructor in his Maryland farmhouse: he is a member of some audience unsuspected, yet he does not understand this language. In the bright kitchen, the following morning, with grapefruit and coffee on the table, I felt an exile, somehow totally out of whatever world I live in, fuzzy and—inexact. On the bookcase, a fly. In the mind, A. Darkness, darkness. Later, another poet would ask me if I had ever met John Crowe Ransom. Poets together. Yet *my* poets—their secret lines speak to me. A poet. A poet. English instructors and their wives. Depressed.

At such times, one throws up a hasty wall of wit and anecdote, behind which the heart can hide. From its retreat, it listens to the spectacular hyperbole rumbling above it. I board the train for home and am again at the beginning. The fields and towns go by, the soured Jersey flats finally. A.

B-b-b-b-b. The sound an idiot makes. I remember Jo-Jo, ah, a perfect idiot name. A Mongoloid, shuffling down the street on the arm of his grey and faded Irish mother, punching himself in the face. Yet we all stand now as idiots in the face of the mass devastation of feeling that abounds. A culture that can give no sustenance, and yet the remedies are for still more "useful skills." Useful skills, and the heart dies, the imagination crippled so that mere boys are become mass murderers or drift blindly into a sterile adulthood. The young, the young! In a stupendous rage of nonbelief—faced with a spurious culture, the art that can give life sullied or made unavailable. What art there is is cheap and false, dedicated to a quick assay of the superficial. Don't believe for a moment that art is a decoration or an emblem. It is what life there is left, though ill-used, ill-used. The young crying for nourishment, and they are given the cynical products of the most fickle market. "Look at what passes for the new," the poet says. Put a handle on it and sell it, cotton candy: to be gone in a moment and leave no memory other than the memory of sickening sweetness.

Well, so the country is dying and against its death I can do—nothing. What little I have to offer, all find useless. A government of scoundrels, a people numb with hatred and fear. Against it, I write, and write what? B? Betty Boop. Boop-boop-a-doop. Babel. Babble. The false poet has written a false novel, the language further corrupted. This rubbish will sour and destroy the soil. I write B. What will put an end to our delighted suicide? I see, I see—a feather of cloud against the azure sky. Or is it deadly smoke from the Con Edison plant? So that even the very clouds are doubted. Instruct the young? In what? The man who goes to live in the commune of love, to worship the soil, and save a small piece, a square foot even, of land, is to be commended. Yet it is true that he has singlehandedly destroyed his children's lives. Yet, God, how he wanted to live! To simply live! At thirty-five, he turns over a new leaf and finds there, dust. A feather of— cloud?—against the azure sky. Vapor trails from a jet over

9

New Mexico. What shall I do, sign a petition? Of course.

"You are a writer? How contemptible. You artists are all alike. It is a blasphemy to write, to cultivate your soul, to seek out beauty in the midst of this injustice. The poem is irrelevant, irrelevant. We do not wish for truth, but for action!"

The poet writes, B. In his despair he insists on its right to be labeled a poem: for what does it matter anyway? B. B. It is a poem, all I wish to give you, he says. He mutters. Not enough, this clamoring audience says, it wants answers, it wants action. The language it employs to make these demands is dead, a smell of putrefaction hangs over it. The poet, idiot of artifact, punches his face, babbles, b-b-b-b.

That's what we like to see! The pig! The language he speaks is indecipherable, untranslatable! That he has achieved an instance of changeless beauty is insupportable to them. Sign this petition, you wretched bastard! Support your local police! Salute the flag! Believe in the schools! And do something!

Do what? It is incredible that he should love his line, and hover over the very commas of it. The wonder is that any artist stays sane. He, whose whole industry is the precise figure, an achievement of grace and daring that have long passed from the world. Do not believe that beauty is not despised. In its natural state it is not tolerated but for carrion statements of the President—who cannot admit that the heart dies in pieces. As an artifact—ah, as an artifact . . . more fuel for the great furnaces of industry.

> The President cannot admit
> that the heart dies
> in pieces: the mode runs
> from red to grey.

> Red to grey.
> Imagine the hearts here
> crisp and crackling
> cellophane.

Above the crimson
fire trucks the streaming
Glory. The walking dead
have little use for it.

The firemen
trust the grimy banner trust
the grimy banner
trust the grimy banner.

We go about our business in the rooms and corridors of the
Splendide-Hôtel. Outside, the black polar night, a chaos of
glaciers. In the ballroom, a false orchestra plays false music
to which all are dancing. In a small suite somewhere in the
rear of the great hotel, the poet has abandoned his egoistic
mumblings and writes a manifesto that all may understand.
Those who loathe and fear the wispiest touch of the beautiful
will rejoice in his new-found relevance, and even more in his
impotence. Thus is he finally honored for the specious, this
dispossessed man whose hated configurations of the imagination now paper the walls. Later, of course, he will go crazy and
be awarded a medal. Let us assume that it will be called the
Medal of Artistic Freedom.

And now the walls are creaking with the weight of the
black glaciers that press upon the darkening hotel. You will
understand that this is a fantasy: poets are excellent at those
and at times are also amusing in their ceaseless babble.

C But will they believe that the sustenance they need is actually available? That they can go out—reach out—and seize it. Take it home.

A loved patina on a cheap brass figurine of a Hindu goddess: whose name I forget. Yet she has the power of the beautiful, divorced, divorced from the powers of her deity. It comes from London, carried across the Atlantic by a friend. I will not get precious about this—one has read so many poems concerning exquisite flowers arranged in vases from—Japan, let's say. What is it about Japan that it has become a metaphor for all those things Americans can't do?

In a C we see: the form of the crab. Or 100. A century, a C-note. Tell the cultured millionaire, please, that I want one of them each week so that I become the true poetic blazon on my time. Glittering, glistering, yellow-gold. Cheap whisky and the rent every month.

When I tried to read a poem to which I had brought at least some measure of my powers they threw paper cups at me —Coca-Cola cups perhaps—and demanded a rock group. The pity of it is that I wasn't even surprised. So, you see, the poet does know his place: outside, where it has always been —and where he belongs, no? Yet one believed once that there was some use for such activity.

There is a remarkable photograph of Lester Young taken just before he died. He is sitting on a bed in his home in Jackson Heights, Queens. He might as well be in Peking or Jackson-town for all the respect his neighbors accord him. He holds a tenor saxophone. On the bed is his clarinet. In his face the subtle imprint of doom.

Believe it when I tell you that there are phrases of the President's that will change your life. He sits, at the end of his life, knowing what he has done. His gifts gone forth on all the winds of the earth. A complete beauty, a sweetness so penetrating—! This is an homage, yes, unabashed. Salute! A salute to the true President of the Republic.

I know a writer who wished his prose to be transparent so that only the movement and growth of his story would be in evidence. What I mean by "story" I leave up to you. Perhaps it is the story the unemployed auto worker tells his friends over red beer. The juke box is playing "Your Cheating Heart," another story. Creatures of myth, tricked out in wool plaid shirts and Sweet-Orr khakis. It is an absolute fact that none of the men in this tavern have ever read Proust or Joyce, nor have they read Rimbaud or Williams. Yet, one of them is telling a story. The movement is traditional, in its way the tale has the delicacy and tension of Forster. The story ends with a quiet grace and one of the men gets up, spits phlegm on the floor, and plays Hank Williams again. They are totally unaware that they are in fashion.

Perhaps it is this story that the writer wanted to tell in his invisible prose? Yet it so turned out that the glasslike surface of his art attained a unique structural grace that signals a style. So is the story subsumed—in the articulation of a man's face under a corduroy cap, this shape against the peeling paint of the tavern wall, the air resonant with the dead singer's voice, etc., etc.

All this is obvious—or is it? One wishes simply to say that the writer cannot escape the words of his story, he cannot escape into an idea at all.

This is a work of criticism.

At the moment the writer realizes he has no ideas he has become an artist. From this point he goes on—or he does not go on. On the other hand, he may avoid the entire issue by affecting a belief in ideas. If this is the case, he may enter the tavern and see the drinkers there as manifestations of an ideological or political set. He brings us the news, the news! Couched in the dead and dying locutions he mistakes for art. There is no talented hack alive who cannot hang an image up at a moment's notice on any wall. Tear them down and smash the glass that protects them! This hotel is full of rotten pictures.

I walk through the world, aging with each step. It is the

only world I have, and I am compelled to accept its raw materials, that is, those materials it is given me to deal with. One must find some structure, even if it be this haphazard one of the alphabet. The excellent pitcher mixes up his deliveries, all of which, however, travel sixty feet, six inches. You will understand that this is a metaphor, a literary device of exceptionally limited use. It may even be dead. For something to be dead in literature means that it will forever persist endemically. Consider typhus or bubonic plague.

It is no use thinking that one might talk with the men in the tavern about these things: they would understand, perhaps, all references to baseball, that most beautiful game. Clear artifact, unsullied by time. Yet, who knows? Some time ago a newspaper ran a headline which was a marvel of verbal sophistication to report on an overwhelming performance by Sandy Koufax: there wasn't a cop in New York whose mind did not perform the most complicated gymnastics—in a flash —to grasp the "story" in a series of subtle poetic connections. The headline read: K-K-K-KOUFAX! The message, being an exquisite shorthand, suffers fiercely when paraphrased. One could see that beautiful pitcher at work a hundred times and still be awestruck by his mastery over the materials given him.

I insist that I do not speak of this game as art, yet it is close to art in that it is so narrowly itself: it does not stand for anything else. It exists outside of metaphor and symbol. Shaped and polished artifact, a game of—nouns and verbs.

It is clear that in the artist's famous poem on the red wheelbarrow the word "glazed" has an adjectival quality: it functions somewhat as a gerund. It has the absolute life of the verb, but still holds the pictorial quality, the image, if you like, of the noun. It gives this remarkable work of art its insistent power over the imagination, its quality of arrested nobility. "Glazed." I take the d of that word as my excuse for this chapter.

It is my opinion as well as that of others that the word *grey* spelled with an e is "greyer" than the same word spelled with an a: *gray*.

Can the poet be correct in assigning the color white to this letter? Admitting, therefore, more light to the word so that it becomes itself lighter, creamier, if you will: on the other side of darkness. The blackness of a. *Gray* holds to itself more black than does *grey*.

One knows, of course, that these are trifles of orthography. Yet, and yet—since there is literally no language without the vowel perhaps this is all not so precious as it seems.

For the sake of the chapter and because it satisfies my desire for structural tension let this letter be white indeed. In his poem the poet speaks of the lances of proud glaciers. These must be those glaciers that rise so majestically—white kings! —in the black polar night in which this great hotel stands. I think of them as being against the Chinese ink of the northern sky, tall and luminous white, jagged and formidable.

This long line spread across the horizon:

Ш Ш

A prolonged scream in the wastes.

White kings. Does the poet speak of the White King in chess? This is a game everyone wishes to play well, so it would seem. There is that something exquisite about it. The White King outside of his white tent in the morning mist. It is perhaps its unabashed anthropomorphism that so fascinates the devotees of this precise game.

> Grey. Gray. Grey.
> Gray. That that
> employs a is blacker
> than that that
>
> employs e which is
> redolent of
> white whose e is silent
> white. White.

Black flies swarm on a white glacier. On white kings. Buzz and circle alertly in rising vapors. All things here are dead but for the flies. A sophisticated creature that has insured its existence by exploiting the products of organic decay.

I learned to play chess—or play *at* chess as the expression goes—from a man in my company in the army. Of the many things I remember about him two come to mind immediately each time I think of him: his love for avocados and his showering in a Mexican bordertown brothel with five whores. I see him there, streaming with soapsuds and water in the whirling steam, he and the girls laughing with enormous joy. He was, I believe, a regional chess champion in his native Pennsylvania.

It would be an enormous pleasure to me if he would read this book—finding it on his own—and recognize himself in it. To open it in his easy chair, his four or five children involved in their various activities, his wife preparing supper. He sits back and takes a swallow of cold beer and suddenly—suddenly he tastes that ripe avocado, lightly salted and tangy with a squeeze of lime and smells the clean flesh of those harsh Mexican whores, sees their white teeth and golden crucifixes. He puts the book down to look across the room at his wife. The aroma of meat loaf in the oven, apple pie with plenty of cinnamon.

Outside, the streets and lawns of Allentown are white with the last snowfall of winter, it comes down with that fabled gentleness all writers at some time remark upon in one way or another. And why not?

Certainly anyone can pinpoint the correspondences and connections in this work, or in any work. What of it? To do so with—what?—love, however, is to be drawn so deeply into the cast of the language that one is left finally with its essence to be set against the world. I agree with all who wish to leave something behind that has the flash of the smallest truth. It is, I admit, sadly, sadly, so much of my life's concern. That minuscule flash, that occasion, has more value than the most staggering evasion by explanation of the real. Who will believe it?

Who, who? They want politics and think it will save them. At best, it gives direction to their numbed desires. But there is no politics but the manipulation of power through language. Thus the latter's constant debasement.

Beauty is but a flowre,
Which wrinckles will devoure,
Brightnesse falls from the ayre,
Queenes have died yong and faire,
Dust hath closde *Helens* eye.
I am sick, I must dye:
    Lord, have mercy on us.

FWell, why speak of children's games? The man is fumbling around, composing, composing. It is perhaps because they are mostly dead except for memory. Or has the composer lost touch with people completely? Yet he walks through the streets, has walked them for years, and sees little to compare with the enormous range of play he once himself knew. Why speak of them? They are there, lucid in the past, fossilized therein. Great sweet flashes, the players stilled.

Can they be thought of as metaphor? Yes, of course—but then anything can be thought of as metaphor. One sees films in which the entire construction of a particular part reveals itself to be a camouflaged scaffolding of metaphor. It is incredible to me that one can devote an entire life to such a precise recording of the unreal. Perhaps it is what keeps actors sane. For I submit that all actors are totally sane, their sometimes bizarre façade is merely another developing role. For myself, when the real is insupportable, I act fairly well, I look the same, I rarely slip into aberrant behavior—yet I think myself to be crazy. At times I have said to myself, aloud, "I must be crazy." The laughter that I release immediately and invariably upon hearing this rubbish brief upon the air is affected and strained—another manifestation of my slipping hold on the normal. I mean to say that when I do go crazy, it is only for a minute or two at a time.

A poem may sometimes open to you, a flower; or it will close up suddenly, a trap, inside a nervous rat, moving in swift jerks. One sees, not the poem, but the poet's absolute intent. Or, the floor unexpectedly opens, and a black underworld is glimpsed. You're better off walking in the mountains. Be sure to bring a book of verse to read after your sandwich and Swiss-chocolate bar. *Une Saison en Enfer* will do nicely.

But the games, the games. One struggles with the metaphor, I mean struggles to avoid it. A list might do it, for many of the names are nondescriptive. If you have never played these games, you will have to be content with the words. In a movie one is forced to show things. I have the privilege here of listing.

Chase the White Horse, Chicken Pull, Dump the Apple Cart, Kick the Cannon to Mexico, Blackwell, Peelaway, Buck-Buck, Ringaleevio, Splendide-Hôtel, Red Rover, A, E, I, O, U, Mumblety-Peg, Boxcars, Milkman, Big Dick, Banker Broker, Voyelles, Shiv, The Clap, Giant Steps, Time, Gunsel, Moldy Fig, TNT, Kick the Can, Chaos de Glaces, Can of Corn, Red Light, Chow, Hide and Seek, The Joint, Johnny Hicks, Stoop Tag, Ballin' the Jack, Rois Blancs, Speedball, Jump Rope, War, Kicking the Gong Around, Follow the Leader, Benny One-Ball, Duke Me, Knuckles, The Hucklebuck, Slope-Out, Twenty-One, Mers Virides, Blues 'n' Bells, Baltimore Chop, Big Natural, GI Party, Now's the Time, Old Maid, Jelly-Jelly, Mouches Éclatantes, Klactoveedsedstene, Steal the Old Man's Bundle, Schlepper, One O'Cat, Texas Leaguer, Little Joe, Sang Craché, In the Bag, Eighty-Six, Catchaflyerup, Divin' for Pearls, Ding-Dong, Snake Eyes, Rayon Violet, Ghosts, Good Soldier, Oleo Strut, Billy McCoy, Alice the Goon, Broken Hearts, Lillabullero, Phoebe, Hello Central, Our Delight, Three Deuces, Blazes Boylan, Hot Beans, Gedunk, Guinea Red, McShanty, Scotch Mist, Fongoo, Oop-Bop-Sh-Bam, Trois Dents, Joe Bush, Hindoo, Mexican Hat, Bread 'n' Buddha, Twenty Grand, Sundae Mass, Acey-Five, Piss-Eyed, Eggies, Coffee And, Métropolitain, Bag o' Skag, Orange Crush, L'Éclair, Dem Bones, Construction, Sheila's Dream, Lock and Load, Prince Albert, Three-Ring Bottoms, Joralemon, Mellowrooni, Medical Dick, Abracadabra, Jamoke, Gussie G, Truckin', O and Two, Butterfly Kisses, Home Free, Potsy, BCD, Mae West, Zoot, Sicilian Vespers, Moxie.

The reader will see that this chapter has little to do with the letter f.

"The Lord succeed my pink borders."

Williams writes:

> And so it comes
> to motor cars—
> which is the son
>
> leaving off the g
> of sunlight and grass—

It seems clear that the poet meant to write the word "song" in the third line of the first stanza, and inadvertently left out the g of that word. One imagines the flash of imagination as he realized his error and then, instead of returning to the line to amend it, saw the possibilities of the poem refreshed. The work takes a new direction, the lost letter reappears audaciously in the next stanza. Yet that lost g is gone from the poem. What if that line had read, as I suspect it was meant to read, "which is the song"?

> And so it comes
> to motor cars—
> which is the song
>
> of metal and glass—

It is that deleted g I wish to concern myself with in this chapter—in one way or another.

G, as the dictionary tells us, was originally a differentiated form of C, the latter identical with the Greek gamma, and the Semitic gimel. C and G, divergent species, one might say, of the same genus. Then consider this irony: Captain Rimbaud and General Aupick.

One recalls the well-known story concerning Charles Baudelaire during the revolutionary upheavals of 1848. At the barricades, an unfired rifle in his hand, wild-eyed, he repeatedly demands that the revolutionists go and shoot the director of the Military Academy, General Aupick, his stepfather. "Down with General Aupick!" This pitifully desperate cry is, for the poet, the extent of his political activity. This February day in Paris, this young man in the streets, for the first and last time at one with the people—here is a symbol of Le Poète that the Master himself would have cherished. It is this artist's work that so deeply influenced that of Captain Rimbaud's son, Arthur, whose first experience with the people was a sexual assault by soldiers. The poem in which this is detailed is called "The Cheated Heart." There are men who stand on my corner in all weathers, drinking beer or wine, who might well have the faces of these brutalizing troops. There is a possibility that they know my name, although they have never read any of my work. They have never heard the name Arthur Rimbaud. Although I do not know for whom I write it is certain that it is not for these men: another dilemma of politics.

General Aupick was an Irish bastard. Captain Rimbaud last saw Arthur when the latter was six, and never again. It is strange to realize that I know more about the sons than their fathers did.

Arthur Rimbaud was at the construction site when the Splendide-Hôtel was built.

H To construct in the imagination the devastation of the small town in rural America. By the letter h? "Rural America" is a phrase hauled gasping and moribund out of Romance.

Forms of death
and destruction. Doom.

Pork Jaw, Mississippi
Belle Aire, Indiana

have neither room
to hide in.

Forms of death
and devastation doom.

With all the glamour of delicate porcelain from Limoges or hand-carved wooden toys for the Christmas stocking, the powerful drug enters the little town, coming in on a Trailways bus or a trunk line of the Texas-Pacific. To parse the sentence with the craft employed thirty years ago will not lessen the attraction of this narcotic. H! H! The populace disappears into an ice-blue mist. Wrap your troubles in dreams. What chance at all against oblivion—?—they are all American boys with their American girls. Rough farmers coming in on Saturday nights in their clay-spattered Ford pickups to get the week's supply. It is to the Emperor Heroin that they finally erect a statue in the middle of the courthouse lawn. The Gift Shoppe on North Main Street (near Matthew Road) seals a few grains each in half-spheres of solid glass and sells them as paperweights. *Souvenir of Buck Forks.*

I don't know why. One week they were playing shuffleboard at Jack's Inn, drinking Schenley and Falstaff, and the next they were at home, searching for a vein. The booze will kill you anyway. Cecil Tyrell falls over from an overdose one day down at the Sunoco station and the Monroe girls—Cora and Janet—are going through his pockets within five minutes, the door to their lime-green Mustang open, their Black Watch tote bags lustrous in the sun.

I clearly remember a place called the Warren House in Hackettstown, New Jersey, some thirty years ago. On the hottest days it was cool and dim, and I remember sitting in the bar on murderous August afternoons, having an orange drink and potato chips while my mother had a glass—a Pilsener glass—of Trommer's draft beer. On Saturday nights, there was dancing and steamed clams with drawn butter in the back room, usually to the music of a small German band that, of course, specialized in polkas. How distinctly I see those sunburned German farmers and their hefty wives flying across the floor. Many of them were members of the German-American Bund and went to meetings in brown shirts and polished boots. Yet they were beautiful on the dance floor. Yet in my tenth year the Warren House was magic. White rockers on the porch in cool shade. Beyond the town the Jenny Jump Mountains, a blue-green haze.

Or one can substitute a different h. The hydrogen bomb. Place that reality in the bloodstream so that the organism is poisoned anew. The Enforcer arrives in the streets of Charleville, Ohio, on a bitter-cold night in January. Kid Blast of international politics. The men from the knitting mills stop off at Henny's Place for just one quick whisky on the way home. Nobody uses the bowling machine anymore. The Kiwanis Fourth of July outing is canceled. Kid Blast, in the best tradition of the movies, is seen sitting in the sheriff's office, smoking his cigars, his feet on the desk. He dials the phone, frowning. God only knows whom he is calling.

The poet says of H: "Sa porte est ouverte à la misère."

In one of the rooms of the Hotel—one which very few of the guests know about—there is laid out a perfect scale model of the American town, ca. 1939. Once I thought I saw myself going into the 5 and 10.

24

 Did the poet not warn us of his later career when he said, "I am the master of silence"? Of course. In this *I* resides his absolute truth. Distrust all people who think that the artist does not mean what he says. For him, for him alone, this stringent letter obeys all commands.

Now, let us assume the installation of the fake, shielded by the letter *I*, behind which, of course, corruption, corruption. The darling of the market composes a novel in the first person "about" the life of Arthur Rimbaud. That is, the narrative —God forgive him—is borne forward by the protagonist: he, Rimbaud, tells the story of his life. The writer, whom I take to be a professional of limited gifts, "writes" *The Illuminations* within the body of this wretched volume. And invents—the Splendide-Hôtel! "I have invented the exquisite figure of the Splendide-Hôtel," he has the poet say. One imagines this comfortable son of a bitch thinking of himself as Arthur Rimbaud. As he places that *I* on the paper he is, in all his mediocrity, more puissant than the shade that he has turned into a "character."

I descend further. Conceive of the idea of some current star of the film world, some "personality," playing Arthur Rimbaud in a movie geared to the expression of Youth in Revolt and Freedom. Ah God! beware the raising of the ghosts of dead poets, damned Catholics hungry for revenge: cadaver of M. Rimbaud drifting toward the set. One imagines starlets running in terror, etc. All those lettuce and tomato sandwiches and containers of yogurt crushed under foot. The director stands petrified in fright, his mouth open: into which buzzes the black A of a fly.

It is that simplest line, that *I* which must be approached with such caution. Of course it is a streak of spat blood, deep red, purple on the sidewalk. Yet it would seem to be the simplest of techniques to handle. It must appear to those who make up the audience as the quickest and easiest way to tell the truth. Merely to tell the truth. Merely! Somehow this first person singular will allow the truth to "escape" the construct of the words. Yet the only literary truth is that construction. Nothing escapes from the writer's words, on the contrary, all things are hammered into them, annealed, fixed forever in rows and rows of the language he composes. To meet Arthur Rimbaud one does not arrange a halfway rendezvous. One boards instead the bus marked L'ENFER.

Purple of the ego, royal purple. The personality of the king, monarch of himself. The purple, we say, purple, ermine, dull sheen of burnished gold, hard-flashing gems and soft luminosity of pearls. The most obtuse of writers wishes to assume this royalty—this purple—by the magical stroke of his pen: to make this simplest letter. "I want to be happy" and "I am the master of silence" are two statements of fact, yet one is rubbish. From the other depends the whole life of an extraordinary man, a particular man, an I. To make such a statement implies a specific damnation.

> In a chaos of glaciers
> and arctic nights
> the Splendide-Hôtel
> was built.
>
> I see poor Arthur there
> another damned Catholic
> what icy passageways
> and muslin trees.
>
> What cardboard seas
> the poet crossed
> to depart his
> purple France.

J is a hook.

When I was sixteen, I caught a largemouthed bass while trolling from a rowboat on a vacationers' lake in New Jersey. The nearest town was Charleville, notable primarily for its fish hatcheries. I was using a small daredevil, hoping, I suppose, to hook one of the pickerel that lay along the shore in the shallows shaded by trees coming down to the edge of the water.

If one looked at this lake at dusk with half-closed eyes it took on the powdery image of that lake in the picture that hung in my hall as a child. This has to do with the past. J is a hook. The future is a bore simply because it hasn't happened.

When the bass struck the lure, I thought for a moment that I had fouled my line on a branch or the trunk of a submerged tree, so powerful and steady was his pressure against me. I pulled against the pressure, thinking to free the lure, when suddenly the line went slack and the bass broke the surface of the water, twisting in spray, rainbows! rainbows!—the image has been fixed by many writers before me. I played him away from the shore and reeled him in, then held him up, quivering and twitching, to my friend, Artie, who was rowing the boat. He must have weighed two and a half pounds.

I never caught another bass with that daredevil, and although I hooked two pickerel with it I lost them both. In subsequent summers I became interested in girls and never game-fished again. From the blankets on which we sprawled I would look across the lake to the shady banks, watching young men fish the shallows. They were incredibly strange, remote from life. I, of course, was at the bloody core of it. Of course.

A daredevil is a spoon lure that comes in three or four different sizes and is intended for daytime fishing. It can be tied to the leader so that it has either a wobbling or a spinning action. The fact that it runs shallow makes it excellent for pickerel. On the convex surface of the spoon the brilliantly enameled design is invariably the same—red with a white stripe running diagonally lengthwise. The concave side is highly polished nickel. From the rear and wider end of the spoon hangs sometimes a treble hook, the points uncovered; sometimes a single hook is rigidly affixed to the lure. This hook is often partially concealed by a wet streamer fly, usually orange in color. It is a beautiful spoon and in action the alternation of the flashing colors and glittering nickel makes it an extremely effective one.

There was a recent news story concerning a researcher working under a large grant from the Department of Health, Education and Welfare. The man, after many tests, discovered that fish can see colors. He discovered that fish can see colors!

J is a hook: to fish up the past: spray and rainbows. My friend Artie later fell in love with a girl who lived on Arthur Avenue in the Bronx. The writer stands transfixed before such gentle irony, notwithstanding the fact that he has invented it.

		TEAM: ALL-STARS (INTERNATIONAL)									
PLAYERS	POS	1	2	3	4	5	6	7	8	9	
LINDSAY	b	K			K			K			
HOOVER	4	63			K			7			
CLEAVER	7	43			x			53			
GUEVARA	2		8			13			x		
NIXON	8		K			x			8		
WALLACE	9		x			x			K		
ROCKEFELLER	3			K			K			x	
McCARTHY	5			K			K			K	
LENIN / KENNEDY 6th	1 / PH			x			K				
MARCUSE 7th / LENNON 9th	1 / PH									K	
TOTALS		0	0	0	0	0	0	0	0	0	

Reproduced above is all that is left of the score card of an
All-Star game played some time ago. It is the section of the
card devoted to the offensive play of the losing team. Unfor-
tunately, none of the players on the winning team are known
at this time, nor is the final score known. It is, of course, apparent that the winning pitcher was a master who must have
here pitched his greatest game.

L In the cellars of the Splendide, there are surely hundreds of rats, few of which are ever seen. One observes the greasy swing marks made by their filthy bodies at those points where beams and pillars join. On occasion, droppings may be seen along their runs. Everything necessary for their survival is here —warmth, shelter, and proximity to food and water. These rats are kings and queens, they are, in a sense, splendid. Ferocious, aggressive, strong and lithe: this is the brown rat, *Mus decumanus*, well-established in Western Europe since 1727, when they swam the Volga in hordes after an earthquake. They make relentless war on neighboring tribes, the members of which they recognize instantly. There are sporadic and halfhearted attempts by the members of the hotel staff to eradicate the rats, but the killing of a few rats simply makes the remaining members of the tribe stronger. One can see the rats waiting in the dense ice of that polar night for the great hotel to be completed, slaughtering their young, cannibalizing each other. Unparalleled except by man in their ferocity.

A rat baffle is designed to thwart a rat's entry into a building through the cellar by confusing his sense of direction. Its shape is that of an L.

> L, the simple shape,
> a baffle for rats
> to go wrong: a jape.

Where the brown rat lives, no other rat may survive. They are xenophobes and patriots from Chinese Mongolia. They can gnaw through wood, concrete, and steel. They attack and kill members of their own species. They wage intertribal war. They kill the female of the species and their own young. They are cannibals. They cannot vomit and so can eat almost anything. They are almost totally blind and "see" with the hairs on the sides of their bodies. They migrate often, bringing with them plague and devastation. They will gnaw off their own legs to get out of a trap. They are utterly destructive of all other forms of life.

30

In the Splendide-Hôtel, there is at least one rat for each guest. This ratio holds true for the world at large. In terror, one can conceive of them all joining together and moving on the cities of the earth. What Chairman's Thought or Senator's reference to Honest Abe will change the mind of one rat? They understand most clearly what men, their supreme natural enemies, also understand most clearly: utter destruction of all other forms of life. I want to know what the President would say should they begin to swim across the Potomac by the millions. A rat is unimpressed by talk of a just peace, he recognizes no flag, and his ideology is food. Food! Food! Swimming across that fouled river, their glittering eyes on the Capitol and the Washington Monument. Meanwhile, the President speaks to the Nation of self-sacrifice and of how shocked he is that France, long our friend and ally—one may say a "natural" ally—should allow these rats to migrate from their homeland. "It has been proven that these rats are directed from the Splendide-Hôtel, a French possession." Therefore, if this massive aggression does not cease we will, however much it pains us, move to "meet that aggression *at its source*." The rats move through those cemetery streets toward the Department of Health, Education and Welfare—none of which they hold in the slightest esteem—and its Rodent Control Section. "Thank you, and good night," the President says and moves to the elevator that will take him to his underground operations center. He never banked on anything like this when he dreamed of power, mowing neighbors' lawns back in Belle Aire, Indiana. He is lucky, indeed, to have the imagination of a sportswriter.

From high in the air the rats swarming over the surface of the earth resemble the fantastic lice of the Comte de Lautréamont. What makes them more terrifically horrifying is that blood is only a small part of their diet. The reader will forgive a whisper of anthropomorphism if I have the leader of the rats shout "May God damn forever all who cry 'Peace!' "

One of the clichés of the time is that the very best men—one speaks of course of men who are "in the news"—are those who have not denied their roots. Wearying columnists with souls of excelsior, blank university presidents, distinguished dullards in every field—all are constantly battering one concerning the splendors of some lackluster politician who still retains traces of a Jersey City accent, who bravely lays into a huge order of scungilli at some restaurant on Elizabeth Street, who puts on a hard hat and screws in a plumbing fixture (badly, of course, as he did when he *was* a plumber). Roots, roots! They address groups of drunken Norwegians in Bay Ridge, tell you of the finer points of bocce, remember fondly those days hustling freight on the North River piers. Somehow, these tenuous connections with their drab backgrounds are commendable.

Let us take the case of Mister, or Monsieur—I shall call him M. Many years ago, he rejected his roots for one reason or another: success in the theatre, the arts, business, politics. As he climbed steadily in his field—we will use the figure of "climbing" since all Americans, even the neurotic dogs they possess, understand this act—he displayed all the finest traits such a success can own. (I grant you that this is fantastic: the idea that a political man, for one, can possess "finest traits" is chimerical. But bear with me for the sake of the conceit.) At some juncture in his life, perhaps at those famous crossroads in that famous Yellow Wood, he decided to take the road that led Back Home.

Years pass. M has rediscovered himself, his heritage, his roots, all the rubbish he was well rid of twenty years before. He is completely whole. And yet, how curious it is, he has become a sham and a fake. By some mysterious law, totally incomprehensible to me, he was a more legitimate figure when he lived his manufactured life. As soon as he became real, he became false. Beware him.

Get out of his way as he speeds back to the People or he will smash you to pieces. There are men who have deserted their wives and children for the People. Beware them, though their actions are couched in the most resplendent rhetoric. Beware the man who tells you of his father's eldest sister's second son —the one who could whittle the most beautiful letter openers. Beware the fake gleam of nostalgia in his eye. Leave the bar when he plays "I Can Dream, Can't I?" Be sure you are behind locked doors when he speaks of Glenn Miller. "While the public funds are spent in celebrations of fraternity . . ." avoid those feasts and block parties, those playground openings for which we have no one but M to thank. "A bell of rose-colored fire tolls in the clouds." How few hear it, yet it continues to toll, despite the museums, parks, and new rides on the midway.

And there is M, getting on the Super Bobsled, which destroys the equilibrium of its passengers to "Sympathy for the Devil." He waves to his constituents, his brothers, shining in a dashiki, a cuchifrito in one hand, a knish in the other, speaking a spicy mixture of Swahili, Yiddish, and Spanish. Move swiftly toward the subway as he pats the mounted patrolman's horse: the bell is tolling, flashes of pink fire in the massed clouds over the ocean. And now a great roar as he salutes the flag, a tear in his eye as he recalls to the throng the great days when it was treated with respect. That must have been about the time we incinerated Dresden.

Dresden! And it so turns out that he remembers Dresden and has some words of wisdom concerning its devastation: "Those who live by the sword," he begins, and his voice is lost in the applause. A drunk in a boat some miles out to sea looks up at what he believes to be thunder and lightning.

N stands for No, the one word that God would utter did He deign to speak. It is the controlling factor of all religion, no matter its protestations of optimism and joy: rightly so. Cleave to the strict beliefs of a fumbling creed or get out of it, get out of it! No, they say, no. Say it along with them and leave the Mass as Art, or the Epistle to Electric Guitar to those who believe in reform—happy men! I believe in the obfuscation of the celebration of God's mysteries, let it remain in Latin, let it be changed to Greek for that matter. It is the business of religion to conceal. Let it molder and stink in its divers closets, inventing those laws of joy it promulgates and upholds.

I love those monstrous religions that shove you into Hell: think of all the priests, policemen, and legislators roasting forever in that catechism inferno, along with the good sisters who beat their childish palms with rulers. And to think that they might possibly have avoided it had they merely disavowed the creed that finally damned them.

When I was a boy I envied all Protestants because it seemed there was no way they could be damned, while I lived all my adolescent years in a state of blackest sin. The Protestants marched in parades, sang hymns, and ate ice cream at church picnics. They changed religions if they disapproved of the minister who attended to their needs. How fantastic to think of the minister as a personality, rather than the surrogate of God. Incredible! In the schoolyards the Roman Catholics, segregated by sex, stood in bitter cold, performing instantly to the signals of the nuns' wooden clappers.

No! No!

Then the children entered the church and the gorgeous decadence of gold, silk, and flowers. A cartoon of heaven. One understood, even then, that the religion was catatonic and was moved about by means of a supreme kitsch. Non-Catholics are delighted by this and think of it as splendor, the Roman ceremonies and sacraments seem to them exquisite, much like beautiful carvings in jade or lapis lazuli. Yet I assure you that they chill one to the bone, they point toward a hell of scorched flesh and endlessly bleeding carcasses, screams and moans of horror forever, forever. They are the No made tangible. While the Protestant Hell is to be eternally unemployed.

One never understood why Protestant children went to church on Sunday, for not to go to church meant nothing. It must have been because of love of Jesus Christ. My religious peers and I went to Mass since to miss Mass was to place oneself in the way of damnation: we went out of absolute fear. It is because of such depravity that Roman Catholicism is a true religion. Catholic children know nothing of Jesus save that he was a vague, bloodless creature whose greatest glory was in allowing himself to be murdered. Their most innocuous sex fantasies seem bestial in the light of this neurotic's warped life. Step clear of it for one cannot reform this insanity by any means whatsoever. Attempts to do so always construct a hale and hearty Jesus, a regular guy—like Father McGrath, who once tried out for the Brooklyn Dodgers.

Arthur Rimbaud received the Sacraments before he died and was damned nonetheless. With what bitterness he must have realized his defeat as the Eucharist was placed on his tongue.

That the entire sky
be the blue gaze
of God's eyes.

In the hollow interior of the O the poet comes upon his figure of the depths of space. With a blue pencil I fill in each o that occurs in the poem as a constant reminder to myself of the artist's invention. Those angels that famously danced on the head of a pin are the same who flash through light years within the boundaries of this letter. It is Rimbaud's imagination that allows us this basically theological perception. Yet nowhere has the Pope revealed that he has even a casual knowledge of this poet's work. It is curious that the King of the Catholics is ignorant of the notes of a fellow Catholic, one who has spent time in Hell.

"The violet ray of Her Eyes." Does he speak of his mother's eyes? Or does he conceive of God to be a woman? He himself has described his own eyes as whitish-blue, the color one sees in photographs of gunfighters and marshals of the Old West, men of violence and death. In the glance of his own eyes in the mirror the poet may have found his line.

Sitting on a stone quay facing the Gulf of Mexico many years ago I wrote an entire novel in my mind, its title, *Blue Ray*. It was, as I remember, a Christmas morning, warm and sunny, the water a bright blue, blue sky. It was, of course, about a young man alone in a Texas Gulf town. The day grew cloudy and chilly and I returned to the hotel with a pint of Paul Jones and read a novel far into the night. At about four in the morning I got up and wrote the title of my novel on a sheet of hotel stationery: I wrote nothing more but soon fell asleep.

Now that I think of it, I realize that the novel's title was just the reverse, *Ray Blue*, the protagonist's name. At just about this time, almost twenty years ago, another young writer was composing a short story called "Mr. Blue."

Let us assume that Raymond Blue is the name of an insurance agent in the Middle West. He has somehow "walked out of the pages"—a reviewer's delight—of my unwritten novel. As he pulls his Chevrolet into the drive-in to get a hamburger and Coke, the author of "Mr. Blue" drives out into the traffic heading toward Indianapolis. Raymond Blue! Mr. Raymond Blue—the invention of my youth. And now he orders a hamburger, with everything. This must be what critics refer to when they say that a writer has created real people.

The "suprême Clairon" the poet refers to is perhaps an example of artistic prescience, i.e., it is a blue trumpet, the horn of, say, Clifford Brown.

A painter whom I have invented has recently painted a picture which, after some deliberation, he has decided to call P. It is not a good painting but I find myself strangely drawn to it. Blue is the predominant color used, and it is applied heavily and without elegance or imagination. The whole effect is one of a striven-for amateurism, or primitivism. One knows that this look is intended to mask the fact that the painter is a man of meager gifts. Yet, and yet, I find myself drawn to this picture.

Two groups of three people each: a man and two women in one group, two women and a man in the other. They are playing croquet on a muddy-blue lawn, blue murk swirling about them. The people seem totally lost and destitute, awkwardly fixed in their blue garments.

The other day I remembered an old photograph that I hadn't looked at in years, and went searching through the house for it. I found it in a file drawer with some other old photos I have kept for one reason or another. It is, of course, a picture of six people playing lawn croquet. The photo is brown and white, but retains a clarity of line that makes it look absolutely new. In terms of structure and composition it is infinitely superior to the painting I have described. The players are grouped exactly as they are in the painting, but their images are sharply delineated. One can clearly make out the expressions on their faces. The figures are posed, yet curiously, they are not stiff, except for one woman, who must be my grandmother: she is holding her mallet as if she is about to strike a ball. The ball, however, is in no position to be struck by her; further, she is not looking at her ball, but at the ball of the young woman who is actually arrested—or so it seems—in the act of striking *her* ball. This flaw in no way spoils the photograph, and, in fact, somehow adds to it a distinction that is never achieved in "candid" snapshots.

The woman who seems to be my grandmother wears a white linen dress. Next to her, a man who looks like my grandfather wears a white shirt, the sleeves rolled to just above the elbows, and white linen trousers. He is intent on

38

the young woman's shot. Beyond the lawn on which they play is a kitchen garden, and beyond that a barn, to the left of which is a smaller outbuilding that might be a garage and tool shed. The shadows fall from right to left. I have studied this picture with a magnifying glass to see if I might discover, from the players' faces, the invisible conversation that is locked into it.

Seeing the painting again after locating the snapshot, I find it poorer than ever. The spurious function that it originally served has been wiped out, having been replaced by the absolute vector of the past. In fact, it has become repulsive to me. What is strange, of course, is how this painter should have come upon his subject, notwithstanding his butchery of it. And why should he call it P? Unless that letter stands for "Photograph." But he knew nothing of the photograph.

Looking again at the photograph I, for some reason, turn it over. On the back, in a hand that is totally unfamiliar to me, someone has written "P."

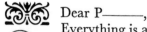 Dear P——————,

Everything is all right here, in many ways, in fact, better than other years, although I look forward to seeing you again. The place seems to be full of rather sinister—I use the word in the "literary" way—people who spend all their time reading Thomas Mann and Hesse, as well as a small "elite" group of what seem to be book reviewers and university professors: they are obsessed with croquet and badminton, both of which they play very badly. After their long, athletic afternoons, they sit in the shade of the porch, rocking, rocking, and getting very drunk on vodka and tonic. Occasionally a heretic or an individualist will drink rye and ginger ale highballs. While the boozing goes on, one can hear the murmur of the endless discussions of Nabokov and Laing.

Arthur is not here yet—of course!—although, as you know, he has promised a dozen times to come for a few days at least. I have heard that he has been delayed for some reason in Batavia. Can that be so? *Batavia?* I have also heard that he has privately published a new book of poems, or prose vignettes—something extraordinarily murky and chaotic, no doubt—but that he has not bothered to put copies in the hands of those who might be of some use to his career. Exactly like him! Actually, I've grown rather tired of his escapades and his "genius" and almost hope that he doesn't come at all. Despite all the bores here, there are a few *very* nice people and I'm afraid that Arthur would feel it his duty to insult them, as usual.

I hate to impose on you, but if you have the time, would you bring me a few books? One grows desperate for reading matter up here, and the only thing resembling a book shop is in the town at the foot of this "mountain," and named after it, Schooleys Mountain. To be generous, it is quite inadequate. After one plows through the thousands of greeting cards of all descriptions, one is lucky to find a shopworn mystery or science-fiction novel. The last one I read was called *Blue Ray*—all about a mysterious ray from Delta 303 that forced people to tell the absolute truth about everything, all the time. It was amusing enough, but the one-note quality of it palled long before the conclusion. In any event, will you be so kind as to bring me these six books, in paper editions if possible. *The Paul Klee Poems*, Jerome Rattenburg; *The Days Rush By Like Freight Cars*, Charles Brzcky; *The Expensive Spread*, Franklyn Newman; *Traprock Ridge*, Lewis Watchung; *The Orange Dress*, Sheila Henry; and *Sanity as Impotence: A Study in Suburban Sexuality*, R. Dilys Canthon. I will, of course, reimburse you for the full cost of these books as soon as you arrive. And, if you have one, bring along a copy of Arthur's new book.

I rush now to conclude this letter, since the first of the post-meridian athletes are mounting the porch steps and soon the hum of alcoholic agreement will drive me to my room.

Be assured I will be waiting for you next Saturday at the DL&W station in Netcong. (I'll be wearing a white carnation, of course!) If Arthur is here by then he may drive down to the station with me. I warn you that you will have to spend your first day telling me everything that has happened in the city this summer. But soft!—the first tray of drinks has arrived on the porch and I must go.

Your friend,

Q

R is a beautiful letter, ultimately deriving from the Phoenician ◁, a tiny pennant. I will it to be an orange pennant, since orange is my favorite color.

Sheila Henry, whose real name is Louise Ashby, wrote the entire first draft of her novel, *The Orange Dress*, during a long summer spent in a cabin in New Jersey's Orange Mountains. This range is also called the Watchung Mountains, by which name Sheila knew it. I offer the reader this intelligence so that he will not be misled into thinking that the name of the mountain range had anything to do with the title of her book. Sheila wrote in great bursts of energy, thirty or forty pages at a time. Interviewed in *The New York Post*, after her book had gone into a second printing before publication, she said: "I write very slowly, and I'm happy to do a good page in a day. *The Orange Dress*, for instance, considering notes and all, took me almost four years to write." The interviewer, lunching with Miss Henry, noted that the author was striking in a pale-orange dress and that she dined lightly but elegantly on a dozen oysters, a white Chablis, and fresh fruit salad. "I have to be careful of my weight," Miss Henry said, "if I want to fit into dresses like this. I love this dress even though it's several centuries old." The interview ended with the author's amused and conspiratorial "orange is my favorite color."

Some Comments on *The Orange Dress*

". . . gives no quarter in its raw account of a damned—and damning—poet's life."—*Jackson Towne*

"The finest account of an artist's life that I have read since *Lust for Life*."—*John Hicks*

"In Cecil Tyrell, Sheila Henry has created a character who can stand alongside Raskolnikov, Flem Snopes, and Yossarian. He lives, he breathes, he walks off the pages!"—*Biggs Richard*

"Plumbs the depths of the artistic soul . . ."—*Léonie Aubois*

SEveryone who is a devotee of graciousness in living knows under what incredibly difficult conditions the Splendide-Hôtel was built: the chaos of ice and polar night, the blizzards and avalanches, the black bitter frosts that took so many workers' lives. Why it was built in such an unprepossessing spot remains a mystery to this day, yet its location has certainly not prevented it from being one of the most elegant hotels to be found anywhere. From the day it was opened in 1872 until the present, it has stood as the epitome of Old World charm.

The Splendide, for many years acknowledged to be the finest hotel in the world, still retains a certain grace and distinction that newer and more overtly luxurious hotels lack. Such touches as the dark-wood paneling and lemon-colored wallpaper of many of its suites, the huge crystal chandeliers of the Golden Age Room, the oiled mahogany and oak furnishings of the Men's Saloon—all assure the guest that he is in one of the very last of the truly *regal* hotels. Although lacking such amenities as a swimming pool and a gymnasium, the Splendide is equipped with almost anything else that a guest may desire: running water, set basins, baths, and showers in every room; palatial water closets, some with wall-to-wall leopard-skin carpeting; steam heat and air conditioning individually controlled by the guest; telephones, televisions, and radios; and enormous feather beds. Contributing to the comfort of the guests are bidets in each room, some of which have been equipped to spray champagne and perfume. The Splendide also operates a laundry, a dry-cleaning plant, an electric-lighting plant, the most modern apparatus for the distillation of water, an ice-making plant, gigantic freezers, and an air-purification center. Among other conveniences are the reading and writing rooms, the library, the music room, the television room, the movie theatre, the coat, package, and baggage rooms, the bordello, the boutique, the barber shops and beauty parlors, the funeral home, the telephone, telegraph, and ticket offices, the newspaper stand, the billiard room, and the limousine and messenger services, not to mention a score of others.

In recent years, the Splendide, while still catering in its inimitable fashion to transient guests, has developed a clientele of "regulars," guests who live permanently at the hotel, and whose names make up a roster of the great and near-great of that age whose splendors have now faded. Among them are Émile Ollivier; Salvatore Rossat, the founder of the Rossat Institute for Colonic Studies; Raphael Menelik; John Baudry; Prince Poniatowski; Barton Kahane; Cora and Janet Monroe; Anton Harley; Giovanni Cazzo; Paul Bourde, the heroin tycoon; Pedro Velasquez; Jacob de Kerdrel; General and Mrs. Maxwell Champagne; Joanne Popsi, the "Darling of the Airwaves"; Jacob Bardey; John Furriskey, Jean Balouche; Leonard DeKalb; "Tab" Jazzetti, the critic; Mr. and Mrs. Leroy Calamari; Booker X; the Baroness Lita D'Ovington; Jeanette Caldecott-Box, the "Heiress to Eros"; Sharon Anne Lingerie; A. C. Ketchum; Isidore Ducasse; the Duke of Coney; Philip and Kelly Gordo; E. Elwood Sprenger; Bartel Pritchard; James Negrón; Paul Shanahan; Curzio Sciaccatano; Harry Humppe, the Presidential advisor; Horace Rosette, the anthologist; Colonel "Buzzer" March; Sir Vyvyan Brier, the drag queen; Ignacio Scallope-Seviche; T. Jane Queynte, President of Dildo International; Antony Lamont; "Tiger" Marconi; Sandra Crotch; the Prince of Orange; Ishmael Melanzana; Senators Joseph Little and Gaylord Nezara; Clark Kant; Van Raalte, "the Garter Belt King"; Nina Caroline; Lance DelRio; Rocky Polenta; Warren "Mr. New Jersey" Hackett; Nathan Famoso; and Monsignor Brad Cannoli. Recently, some of the rooms in the rear of the Splendide have been opened for the first time in fifty years, to allow for the influx of young sophisticates who flock to the hotel on weekends all year round. While it is clear that these young professionals of the advertising, design, and publishing worlds think of the Splendide as the ultimate in camp, the great hotel takes them all in its stride, as it has always taken everything. It may be interesting to note here that in one of the newly opened rooms the following poem, signed by one "Henri Kink" was found in a copy of Monge's *Les Constructions métalliques* that had been tucked away in a bureau drawer.

I read that in a ship's log book, t stands for "thunder."

T Is it possible that this thunder is actually the bell of rose-colored fire tolling in the clouds?

The President cannot hear it, although he is said to be a man who takes care to cross all his t's. Yet he cannot hear this tolling bell. That is because the President is not a man of imagination—how could he be when he does not himself exist outside the imagination of—of whom? Of, let us say, Wallace Stevens. Stevens is a true President of this Republic. The man who is held, shimmering, in the poet's imagination, this man, with his paired cheetahs, his long sideburns and flowered shirts, his beautiful dinner companions, is no one at all. How could he hear that tolling bell?

He has apples on the table. Yet I am sick of him. He drives fast cars and plays squash with a kind of satanic brilliance. One tires of him. He has made his plain face, by dint of cosmetology and a constant, wry smile, the face of all relevant people everywhere: yet the poet in whose mind he lives has the face of a corporation executive—or of a President. He ordains the bee to be immortal, in a ringing speech, available on record and tape. Yet the memory of the sound of his voice is absolute ennui. Since he is constantly talking, dancing, laughing, he cannot hear the bell tolling in the clouds high above him. Bell of rose-colored fire.

His language is that of instruction booklets on the installation of air conditioners. In his more elegantly turned phrases, one hears the echoes of commercials. In his famous speech in which he ordained the bee to be immortal, a hint, a merest touch of press-agentry was apparent. I sicken of him.

I am sick of the Great Books he reads, of his Porsche, his blue-point Siamese cats, his tie-dyed shirts. I am sick of his trout fishing, his hand-tied flies, his shooting the rapids of the Colorado River. I want to remove myself from all talk of his distinguished war record. What is one to make of his attentions to Sheila Henry, the young novelist? What of his love for the Rolling Stones? He reads Marx, Aristotle, Lenin, St. Thomas, he is at the opening of every Godard film. One feels the stomach gripe and churn with nausea. His taste for Sazeracs depresses me. His understanding of the drug culture makes me bone weary. He laughs, he dances, ah God, how he can dance! The bell rings louder and louder. The lightning flashes distantly rose-red.

He has no style. He has all the best styles, the best that can be bought or imitated, at his finger tips, yet he, himself, has no style. The poet has created him, has placed him in office, surrounded by luxurious carpetings and lustrous furniture. On the table a bowl of perfect Northern Spies and Golden Delicious, arranged to perfection. What can one think about the hangman's noose he fashions from the cord of the Venetian blind on the window behind his desk? That very night he attends a Joe Cocker concert at the Fillmore East glorious in a white suit and bright orange shirt and tie. I sit heavily thinking of him. He has no style, yet he claps the time to a t. He reads the underground press, and is concerned with its opinions of him. His underwear is silk, except when he dons faded Levis, on which occasions he wears no underwear at all. He is carefully responsive to the demands of Black Liberation and Women's Liberation. The nausea floods over me.

And what of the barefoot servants round him? Clearly homosexuals, they are given every courtesy by this wondrous man, this exquisite sketch. On the night when everyone in Washington was deafened by the tolling of the bell, the President watched W. C. Fields in *It's a Gift*. He is a great fan of Fields, and of Chaplin, Keaton, Welles, Fellini, Antonioni, and each week, as well, watches at least a dozen underground films—Warhol, the Kuchar Brothers, Mekas, Brakhage, Anger, Vanderbeek, Rice. A patron of the arts, he supports every symphony, dance company, and theatre group in America. He reads poetry constantly, he is well versed in the new fiction, he subscribes to *Art News*, *Rolling Stone*, and *Dance*. Yet, and yet, I am sick of him.

He has no style. He has apples on the table. No one before him ever thought of ordaining the bee, the lowly bee, to be immortal. The servants, each day, adjust the curtains in his office to a t: to a metaphysical t.

I take Rimbaud's animals in the peaceful sea of green pastures to be cows, gentle Guernseys and Holsteins motionless in the stunning heat of July. One sits on the crumbling stone steps of the old white church in its shade, looking out across the lush and variously planted fields going off toward the horizon where there lies a ridge of bluish mountains, above them flashes of lightning and slow, ragged thunder. The cows scattered about, ruminating, and beyond them the farmer on his cultivator bent low, speaking to the two blind horses, Tom and Jim. The long, uncut grass in the churchyard rustles in the heavy afternoon breeze, from the house come muted sounds from the kitchen as the farmer's wife does the dinner dishes and prepares the supper.

One would almost think that in this peace there is some sort of truth.

And now the farmer is beneath the tree in the side yard, sitting at the circular wooden table, his sweaty leather-peaked cap before him, his hand around a bottle of cold beer. He smokes his pipe, looking up at the sky through the leaves. Far away, above the mountains, the sky is dark, it is raining hard at the Delaware Water Gap.

The farmer will die this coming autumn in a fall from the hayloft. The farm will be sold and houses built over all these fields. What I want is for all of this to be stilled, forever. Let the croquet game on the lawn be frozen, let each insect flying against the screens be held immovable. Yet these pastures are the sea. It is all the sea, endlessly moving, endlessly the same. Green. One would almost think that in this peace there is some sort of truth.

I once knew a woman who, gazing at the sea each day throughout a long summer, decided that it had commanded her to change her life, which she did. She is dead now. I see her occasionally on the street, she stares at me with blank green eyes. "Soñando en la mar amarga." The bitter sea, dreaming of the bitter sea. Yet before she invited the sea's destruction her life brought her no peace. Into the empty place that was

V Image of V. Imagine it then on a huge banner, red, white, and blue, of course, streaming arrogantly above the Splendide. The letter stands for Victory, nothing else but Victory. It is a simple scene, one without people, a color post card, on the reverse side a friendly and inane message such as post cards require.

You will understand that this is an old post card that some-one found in a drawer and decided to use as a joke. Let us assume the writer thinks of it as a joke, in any event. But it is no joke at all. The past is inviolate and cannot be hauled into the present to be changed by sophisticated tinkering.

"Dear Van,

We're here for three or four days 'seeing the sights' the only interesting one being this really MARVELOUS old hotel. Other than that, it is bad food and lots of sun. Then on to Barcelona! See you soon—keep well!

xxxx Nina C"

In the days when the great patriotic V flew over the hotel the ballroom was crowded every night with women whose men had gone off to that war whose purpose was to free all man-kind from tyranny, repression, imperialism, colonialism, and hatred. Another blague of history. The men with whom they danced and flirted, and who flirted with them in return, had luckily escaped the general slaughter, or had been to it and returned, their hair grey with terror. They danced each night to the music of Curt Clef and his Syncopated Smoothies, who played such favorites as *God Bless America, Ballad for Americans, The Last Time I Saw Paris, He Wears a Pair of Silver Wings, There'll Be Bluebirds over the White Cliffs of Dover, We Did It Before and We Can Do It Again, Don't Sit under The Apple Tree with Anyone Else but Me, I Left My Heart at the Stage Door Canteen, Praise the Lord and Pass the Ammunition, This is the Army, Mister Jones, Warsaw Concerto, With My Head in the Clouds, You'd Be So Nice to Come Home To, Comin' in on a Wing and a Prayer, Goodbye Sue, No Love, No Nothing, They're Either*

Too Young or Too Old, What Do You Do in The Infantry?, *Bell Bottom Trousers*, *I'll Walk Alone*, and *Dig You Later*; other oft-requested tunes included *Kill The Yellow Rats, I'm Dating Mary Fist Tonight, Hot Pants Samba, I'm Trooey to Yooey, My Second Looey, I Don't Give a Damn if I Die for Freedom, Watch Those Jappies Run, I'm Dreaming of You in Black Stockings, There's Nothing Fey 'Bout the USA, I'm Making Believe Your Two-Way Stretch Is You, Frig for Freedom, I'll Linger on My Finger, G.I. Joe, Jesus Joined the Artillery:Boom, Boom, Boom!, That Red Cross Angel Double-Crossed My Heart, We're Here to Knock the 'ell out of Lasagne, It's Gonna Turn Darn Sour for the Krauts, Don't Kiss That 4-F Bastard on the Doorstep, My Hunk of Dream is a United States Marine, Last Night I Saw Your Face Amid the Flak, I've Got Your Panties in My Old Kit Bag, The Honey on My Biscuit Makes Me Think About You, Let's Send a Million Huns to Hell, Nervous From The Service, The Dildo Boogie, It's Hard to Dance With a Photograph*, and *I Wash My Pillow Every Night With Tears.*

Dancing, crowded, on the dark floor of that ballroom, drunk and lascivious, pelvis to pelvis, the men straining against the maddening rigidity of the foundation garments the women wore beneath their clothing. Many of the men had embarrassing accidents right there on the dance floor, the women smiling sweetly and understandingly into their faces collapsing in anguished and helpless pleasure: subtle flirtation, almost infidelity, the slowly revolving discs of colored lights swimming among the dancers imposing romance on the entire tableau. The management was permissive concerning these activities, so long as things were kept discreetly within bounds, i.e., indecent exposure was frowned upon, onanism at the tables of the cocktail lounge was politely but firmly repressed, and, in one instance that is legendary, a personage no less august than Lieutenant Colonel Maxwell Champagne was roughly ejected from the bar while in the process of "forcing" a Miss C——— to perform an unnatural act on him. Yet basically, it was a policy of "anything goes" —so long as "anything" was reasonably concealed. It was all for Victory.

52

In the black frigid winds above the hotel's revelry, the banner snapped and fluttered.

Here are two exhibits from the time, which may assist the reader in understanding how it was that a beleaguered people, totally unprepared for war, and essentially peace-loving, fought through to ultimate Victory. The first is a brief letter from a young woman to her husband at the front, the second an excerpt from the diary of a C-Ration manufacturer. It may be useful to note that both were guests of the Splendide when these were written.

"My dear Arthur,

I don't know what you mean by me keeping my legs closed. That's a hell of a thing to say to me when you're God knows where f———— everything that moves. And I have my career to think about too! You don't think I'm going to throw that away just because you want to be some kind of a hero. I auditioned last week for Mr. Kink—that's *Henri* Kink —and he said that with a little more polishing the act might easily get a spot on the U.S. Beaverboard Hour. Now, I know what you're thinking, but Mr. Kink and I just had a business lunch *with* his secretary present.

"Janie Queynte and I had a great pizza last night at Culo's and then took in *Wake Island.* I wouldn't mind if you died like that! Brian Donlevy was a peach in it.

"The hotel has a big Victory banner flying over it next to the American flag and it looks great. The manager says it's the biggest Victory banner outside of the one on the Capitol in Charleville.

"I see your mother now and then—she's always butting into my business. Why the heck don't you write her so that she'll stop asking me about you? She gives me a pain. Did you make corporal yet? That's not much money you send me, you know. I need a new dress and nylons *once* in a while.

With love (and my legs *closed*, you rat),

Joanne"

53

"Finally realized why I'm making out with all these young wives. I subtly let them know that I can produce, that I can 'get it up.' Most of the other guys here are impotent, or something, and I have a real masculine look. Something in my eyes. The other day when I looked into the eyes of that Sandi —a terrific broad!—I knew, and she knew too, that we're going to make out together. It's nice to have that kind of insurance for a rainy day . . ."

Years ago, while digging up a garden, I found an old V For Victory button buried in the earth. It was rusted and stained by its years in the soil, but the design and colors were still apparent. I could hear the cracking of the banner in those polar winds and smell the millions of corpses slowly decomposing. V is for Victory, nothing else but Victory.

It is only by persistence that the imagination is freed in order that it may create anything: the Splendide-Hôtel, for example. This hotel was invented by Arthur Rimbaud who later went to live there. I have it on good authority that there are very few people who are interested in this fact. For that matter, a magnificently aware and intelligent couple I recently met—their apparel was forcefully, aggressively even, imaginative—had never heard of the Splendide. They spoke to me of the flowers that they grew in profusion in their small backyard garden. They seemed inordinately proud of them, almost as if they had made them. When I lightly mentioned that Rimbaud had questioned whether a flower, dead or alive, was worth the droppings of one sea bird, they became angry with me, and, I take it, with Rimbaud. The products of the imagination must be tendered with the greatest of care.

Curiously enough, this couple loved the Rimbaud who called for a disordering of all the senses, who spat on priests and flung his lousy body on Mme. Verlaine's bed. In these external "realities" they purported to see the artist. So that the artist becomes a waiter who deftly and unobtrusively serves what is ordered. I agree that the artist as waiter is a fanciful metaphor, yet it leads me to something.

An artist whom I have known for fifteen years has for some time been painting and drawing pictures of waiters arrested in the varied aspects of their work. These are profoundly moving pictures of desperate men, locked into a profession that offers little succor. They are totally beaten, thoroughly defeated, yet they manage to perform their duties with a bravado that is nothing short of heroic. The expressions and postures of the waiters are tragic, they stand, staring out of the pictures, their faces acute delineations of pain and humiliation. Some of them rush through the space of the pictures, trays above their heads, in a shower of falling china, glasses, and silverware. Some lean against each other in exhaustion. Some stand, immobile, trays under arms, blowing smoke rings. And others, wild-eyed, fling their arms and legs about uncontrollably. It is, I think, safe to say that they are all on the edge of insanity.

Nowhere does one see a diner.

I assure you that these are not "real" waiters. They are the waiters of the artist's imagination. They are devastating, they make one uncomfortable, they are totally unlike any waiters that anyone will ever see. And yet—and yet surely they must be the waiters employed by the Splendide. By an act of the imagination, the artist has driven through the apparent niceties of restaurant dining to reveal the bewildered rage and madness therein. One who has seen these pictures can never again dine out without suspecting that the waiters are all involved in a terrific charade. Their irrational behavior and broken spirits *do* exist: in the imagination, purified against all change: in the Splendide. These clearly constructed figures of despair, willed into existence by an act of the imagination, allow us to "read" the activities of "real" waiters acutely. They stand revealed. This subtlety is the artist's entire achievement. Through the employment of the imagination he lays bare the mundane. The painter, who may have seen the necessity for his project in the brief, single turn of a waiter's wrist, must certainly agree with the poet who writes, in a work specifically concerned with the imagination:

> It is only in isolate flecks that
> something
> is given off

So I come again to Williams, another w for this chapter.

William Carlos Williams was eight years old when Arthur Rimbaud died. It pleases me to see a slender but absolute continuity between the work of the damned Frenchman and the patronized American.

X Honeymooners, delirious in the pleasure of each other's flesh, at one time flaunted the legality of their passions by sending post cards of the hotel they stayed at to relatives and acquaintances. An innocent and delicious pastime, now certainly mocked. The messages, silly yet covertly sexual, were always jointly signed. On the face of each card, the windows of the suite in which the couple stayed were boldly inked over with X's. It was as if the newlyweds wished to rivet the attention to these windows, to clearly fix the fact that a glance through them would reveal their abandoned carnality. So that each recipient became an accomplice, a voyeur.

Years later, if confronted with these post cards, the husband and wife themselves discover that they are looking through the windows intently, astounded at the vigor and beauty of the young lovers within, joyous and dazed in their satisfied lust.

> Who is not sensitive
> to the poignance of the splendid
>
> demolished hotel serene
> on some old post card?
>
>> It seems to float in
>> grandeur in the enameled blue
>> that surrounds it
>>
>> old autos speckle
>> the golden streets
>> it looks out on.
>
> On an upper floor
> two black X's
>
> commemorate a honeymoon
> spent behind those windows.

Crushingly sad.
As if this harshest letter
can anneal forever

the lust careened into
and satisfied at last.
It is merely slick paper

which on the reverse side
holds a brief voice

at once sexual and wholly
innocent.

Nothing for eyes to do
but stare at the shining photo
that marks a time completely

gone: this custom is gauche now
and rarely observed
by anyone

Let me say—why not?—that yellow is the color of love. The reader may ask what I know of love, but I confront him with the same question. Unbendingly singular, almost harshly narrow, love—as it spreads out to encompass more and more—loses its power. So that a man who speaks of love speaks of his own meager handful of experiences with it—or of what passes for it. Abstract love, that love which powers religion and philosophy, has less to recommend it than the simple word that occurs over and over again in popular songs. Which, however, offer no solution to the bewildered lover. To love is to go consistently into the dark, perhaps even whistling. All the songs, poems, and novels that the mind drags with it testify to the fact that others are there in the blackness as well: sighing, groaning, or as it may be, howling. Yet the recording of these testaments goes on. We will never be done with it.

The poet says:

> the stain of love
> is upon the world!
> Yellow, yellow, yellow

—so I can claim a "precedent" for my assertion. It may be, though, that in flailing about, the notion that yellow is love's color appealed to my sense of design. I think of the pale sun that occasionally shines above the massive hotel: I think of Amarillo: I think of the color of the walls in that tavern where the men still sit, drinking red beer. The peeling paint of those walls, a kind of dull mustard-yellow, is close to the color I envision. Nothing spectacularly brilliant will do. The color is somehow perversely pleasing in its apposition to that which it surrounds. The men are caught within love itself, and play a song that details one of its facets.

Then, too, I approach the end of my book. I complete the structure as best I can. In a sense, this is the end of the work.

Everyone is asleep in the Splendide-Hôtel.

An Afterword

I've been trying to pay respects to this work since first reading it in someone else's home, in that curious disjunct that made it theirs and not mine despite I was a person of its text and was probably more there, "heading toward Indianapolis," than I was even in reading it. I too loved Rimbaud, that wildly youthful genius who had changed all of French poetry forever before he was even twenty years old. I pondered his "Voyelles" and tried, in careful manner, to deracinate all my senses. In the early 1940s, with the whole world blowing up around us, it seemed a sufficiently modest proposal. So I note with interest that *Splendide-Hôtel* was first published just about one hundred years after the first of the *Illuminations* were written.

Albeit there are many presences in this remarkably particular book, the two who make context for the imagination it "so much depends upon" are, of course, Arthur Rimbaud and William Carlos Williams, and Gilbert Sorrentino's homage to Williams's authority is always emphatic: " 'Look at what passes for the new,' the poet says." Rimbaud is source for the title, both it and the motto being taken from the first of the texts in *Illuminations,* "Après le Déluge," in which "As soon as the idea of the Deluge had subsided," there begins a divers coincidence of actions, some sophisticated and reflective and some of primal innocence. "Caravans set out. And Hotel Splendid was built in the chaos of ice and of the polar night." Or as Sorrentino writes in his second sentence: "Thus, any story." It is in just so simply *seeming* a manner that words become the reality we had only believed them to be issue of.

Rimbaud's heroic definition of the artist previously mentioned would be immensely attractive in itself, but even more to be valued—' as one thinks of the hundred years—is the formal improvisation he was able to make hold against the canons of French literary style. Baudelaire's *Paris Spleen,* which one presumes him to have known, would be a useful precedent, but it does not anticipate the genius of his own invention or the impact it will have on *all* formal device in French poetry. "For Rimbaud," as John Porter Houston aptly says in

The Design of Rimbaud's Poetry (1963), "a style is a system suited to a specific poetic conception and not to an author's characteristic mode of expression."

With that useful point in mind, one can then judge the parallel of Williams's situation in the composition of *Kora in Hell* (1920) or the *Improvisations,* as he also calls them:

> I let the imagination have its own way to see if it could save itself. Something very definite came of it. I found myself alleviated but most important I began there and then to revalue experience, to understand what I was at— *(Spring and All,* IX, 1923)

Ezra Pound's response was wryly abrupt: "But what the French *real reader* would say to your *Improvisations* is Voui, g(h)a j(h)ai déjà (f)vu g(h)a g(h)a c'est de R(h)imb(h)aud!!" The quotation comes from Stephen Fredman's *Poet's Prose* (1983) and is used, paradoxically, to emphasize that Williams did *not* know Rimbaud's work specifically—or, to quote another of Fredman's sources, Mike Weaver: ". . . as Williams informed René Taupin, his knowledge of French culture was visual and not literary."

So it is, curiously enough, Gilbert Sorrentino who serves as their introduction in many ways indeed. As one might well expect, the factors and habits of his attention are solidly American, as are Williams's. Thus Rimbaud's *A* in "Voyelles" ("black hairy corset of the bursting flies which buzz around the cruel stench, gulfs of shadow") becomes ground for more thoughtful consideration in Sorrentino: "On the bookcase, a fly. In the mind, A."

So too the *d* of the word "glazed" in that most familiar of all Williams's poems:

> so much depends
> upon
>
> a red wheel
> barrow
>
> glazed with rain
> water
>
> beside the white
> chickens

"I take the d of that word as my excuse for this chapter" ("D")—which has been at such pains to separate writing from the simple excuse of an intention. "One wishes to say simply that the writer cannot escape the words of his story, he cannot escape into an idea at all."

Neither can he escape the compacted habit his life has been given. "I walk through the world, aging with each step. It is the only world I have, and I am compelled to accept its raw materials, that is, those materials it is given me to deal with. One must find some structure, even if it be this haphazard one of the alphabet." There is no securing point, no compelling and relieving reason. Yet, as with Williams, he knows the perfect: "K-K-K-KOUFAX!"

There is also the *moral* of the writing, any writing, that he shares with Williams, "the government of words." "They want politics and think it will save them. At best, it gives direction to their numbed desires. But there is no politics but the manipulation of power through language. Thus the latter's constant debasement." So it is that the "President" is simply a figure precise to an imagination and conduct, "who takes care to cross all his t's. Yet he cannot hear this tolling bell." Or, "the true President of the Republic," Lester Young. The Prez. "He holds a tenor saxophone. On the bed is his clarinet." For *C*.

But all this seems to have been said, or about to be, in that such work as this takes one far beyond the limits of a prescription. Always something, like they say. Always room for one more.

ROBERT CREELEY